Ghosts in the Night

A huge, bright moon shone through the window, making shadows all over her bedroom. Caitlin held her breath. She'd never before seen a moon that big. Or that bright.

The night was quiet. Very quiet. An owl hooted, startling her. She heard rustling, and a sound like voices sighing. That had to be the wind. Or could it be the spirits of those long-dead Indians?

Then she heard a cracking noise, as though a large animal were stepping on twigs as it hurried through the brush. And heavy breathing.

Caitlin knew she should get up and look out the window, but she was afraid. What if it really *was* spirits?

MYSTERY OF THE
SPOOKY
SHADOW

MYSTERY OF THE
SPOOKY SHADOW

by Gloria Skurzynski & Alane Ferguson

illustrated by Jeffrey Lindberg

Troll

Text copyright © 1996 by Gloria Skurzynski and Alane Ferguson.
Cover illustration by Jeffrey Lindberg. Copyright © 1996 by Troll Communications L.L.C.

Published by Troll Communications L.L.C.

Printed in the United States of America.

10 9 8 7 6 5 4 3 2 1

CHAPTER

1

"Caitlin, you are just a regular third-grade girl. I'm a movie star. Give *me* the good life jacket!"

"Forget it!" Caitlin told Reese Borden.

Reese flipped his blond hair out of his blue eyes. "I don't want to get in that old rowboat in a ratty life jacket," he said.

"So? I got this one first!" Caitlin Marsh tugged the strap of the bright orange life vest, tightening it across her chest.

"Come on, you two, get in the boat," Mr. Mahoney called out. He was the science teacher at Three Peaks Elementary School, and he'd organized this field trip for the Three Peaks Science Club members. "We have to stay on schedule."

Caitlin climbed into the rowboat. Behind her, Reese was muttering, "If something happens to me, I won't be able to star in my next movie, *Dungeons*." Reese really was in the movies—and he made sure everyone knew it. When he wasn't making movies, Reese's parents sent him to Three Peaks Elementary School because they wanted him to be with regular kids and not become a Hollywood brat. So far, being with regular kids hadn't made Reese any less bratty.

The boat wobbled in the water. Caitlin sat down hard. When she grabbed the seat to steady herself, her hand landed on a huge black spider.

"Ha ha, very funny," she said to Pablo Miramontes. Caitlin knew Pablo had to be the one who'd put the plastic spider on the seat, because he was always playing stupid jokes on people. She picked up the spider to throw it back at Pablo, but it missed him. Instead, the spider landed on Reese, who was climbing into the boat.

"Aaaaah!" Reese yelled as the spider fell inside his life jacket. "Help! Get this thing off me! It's poison!" He started waving his arms around so hard, the boat swayed dangerously from side to side. "Get it off! Get it off! GET IT OFF!" he yelled.

"Reese, *sit down*!" Mr. Mahoney cried. "You'll capsize the boat."

"Reese, it's *fake*!" Caitlin shouted, sure the boat was going to tip over and dump them all into the lake.

Reese's mouth was wide open, ready for another scream. Slowly his mouth closed, and his eyebrows sank back from high up on his forehead to just above his eyes, where they belonged. He sat down, dangled the spider by one leg, and said, "You guys didn't scare me. I knew all along it wasn't real."

"Yeah, right," Pablo said. "Sure you did."

"I was just acting," he said. The color began to

come back into his face. "Admit it—am I a great actor, or what?"

From the second rowboat, a voice called out, "What's going on over there? Are you people ready to cast off?"

The voice belonged to Mr. Stan Wiley, who owned both boats. He also owned the ranch on this side of the lake.

"Ready," Mr. Mahoney answered. "Pablo, grab the rope off the piling. Everyone else, sit still!" The teacher began to row, puffing a little as he pulled on the oars. The boat slid out onto the lake. As they moved smoothly through the water, the dock became smaller and smaller behind them.

This was fun! Caitlin liked sitting in the boat with her teacher and classmates. Besides Reese and Pablo, there was Kevin Running Fox, a quiet boy who wore his dark hair long. Kevin and Reese began to play a game of ticktacktoe.

The water made little slapping sounds against the sides of the boat as it glided across the small, pretty lake. Once they reached the other side, the Science Club members would begin their hike along the nature trail, where they'd learn all about trees.

Caitlin's only disappointment was that Joe Daniel Giles happened to be riding in the other boat. Joe Daniel was her best friend, although he probably didn't know that. They lived near each other—Caitlin and her mother rented a trailer space on the Giles ranch. Every morning Joe Daniel and Caitlin waited together at the school bus stop, and while they waited, they talked to each other. But once they got on the bus, Joe Daniel sat with the big boys in the back.

Caitlin understood this—a sixth-grade boy like Joe Daniel would never sit with a third-grade girl like Caitlin. She'd hoped that on this field trip they would at least be in the same boat, but it hadn't turned out that way. Oh, well, she thought. Maybe on the way back.

Puffy white clouds were reflected on the lake's smooth surface. Caitlin let her hand trail in the water. Ripples made by her hand ruffled the cloud reflections and blended into the wider ripples the rowboat made, which spread out behind them like a fan.

"Look at that, Pablo," she said.

"Look at what?"

"The sunlight on the water ahead of us. It's like our boat is sailing right through the sun's path."

"Yeah. Nice," Pablo said without much interest. He went back to reading a book titled *100 Great Practical Jokes to Play on Your Friends.*

"Kids, I want you to pay attention," Mr. Mahoney began. "Once we step off this boat on the opposite shore, we'll be on government land. Mr. Wiley owns the ranch land behind us, but all the land on the east side of this lake belongs to the Forest Service."

"What does that mean, government land?" Caitlin asked him.

Mr. Mahoney cleared his throat. He always did that when he was about to tell them something important. He was a natural-born teacher, Caitlin had heard her mother say. There was nothing Mr. Mahoney liked better than to share information with his students.

"Government land," he began, panting a little as he tried to talk and row at the same time, "is land that our government has set aside for the use of all people. It's where any of us can go to be alone with nature. It belongs to all the citizens of our country."

"Not true!" Kevin Running Fox spoke quietly, but everyone heard him. "This land really belongs to *my* people," he said.

Surprised, Caitlin whirled around to stare at Kevin.

"Yes, your people and all the rest of us," Mr. Mahoney said.

Caitlin wanted to ask Kevin just exactly who his people were, and why he thought the land belonged to them. She knew Kevin was an American Indian, but he'd never before talked this way. She was just about to ask him to explain when Mr. Mahoney announced, "Heads up, everyone. Keep your hands inside the boat. We're ready to land."

CHAPTER

2

Mr. Mahoney jumped into the shallow water and pulled the boat onto the bank. Everyone else stepped onto dry land. When the second rowboat came close enough, Joe Daniel tossed its rope to Mr. Mahoney, who pulled that boat onto the bank, too. Lily Kato had ridden in the second boat along with Joe Daniel, Mr. Wiley, and all the Science Club members' backpacks. Lily was a third grader like Caitlin.

"Everybody here?" Mr. Mahoney asked, although he could see that everybody was. Caitlin liked Mr. Mahoney. He was young—about the same age as Caitlin's mother, who was twenty-nine. His cheeks were round and ruddy. He tried always to be fair, to be a "straight shooter," as he put it. But sometimes he asked silly questions, like "Everybody here?"

"We're all here," they answered.

"Take off your life jackets, stack them on the bank, and gather around," he told them. "We need to talk about rules."

The six members of the Three Peaks Science Club

who had come on this field trip made a circle around Mr. Mahoney as he talked to them. The circle looked like an uneven picket fence, because some of the kids were short, like Lily Kato. Others, like Joe Daniel Giles, were tall.

"We've come to study the ecology of forests," their teacher began. "We're not going to break off any branches, or pick any flowers, or disturb any living thing. Just as important, we're not going to leave any trash around. In fact, if you see trash that other people have dropped, pick it up and carry it out."

Reese Borden muttered, "No way! I'm not picking up anybody else's garbage."

Well, I will, Caitlin thought to herself. This place is so beautiful that I want to keep it clean.

"Let's get going, then, boys and girls," Mr. Mahoney said. "Follow me, stay on the trail, and keep together. Mr. Wiley, do you want to come with us on our nature hike?"

"Not interested," the rancher answered. "I'll wait here till you get back." Mr. Wiley had rented his rowboats to the Science Club. Since each boat had to be rowed by an adult, he'd agreed to cross the lake with them, but that was all.

"All right. We'll return exactly at three-fifteen," Mr. Mahoney promised.

They began their hike, taking a path through the trees. Much to Caitlin's surprise, she found herself next to Joe Daniel. She was delighted when he started to talk to her.

"Mr. Wiley says Mr. Mahoney is a Greenie," Joe Daniel said.

"What's a Greenie?" Caitlin asked. She knew what a Brownie was—she'd been in a Brownie troop until the leader moved away—but she'd never heard of a Greenie.

"You know, someone who loves trees and the environment."

"Doesn't everyone?" Caitlin asked.

"Mr. Wiley doesn't! You should have heard him talking in the boat. He says environmentalists want to take land away from the ranchers. He says the government wants to take the land away, too. He says that cattle ought to be able to graze anywhere at all."

"Oh." Caitlin didn't care about ranchers and Greenies fighting over land. All she cared about was walking next to Joe Daniel under the tall pine trees, along the trail made soft by fallen pine needles, in this national forest that smelled so good. Birds chirped over their heads. When Caitlin looked up to hunt for the birds, she noticed how beautifully blue the sky was. When she stopped looking for birds, Joe Daniel was no longer beside her. He'd dropped back to walk with Pablo.

Caitlin took big steps so she could catch up to Mr. Mahoney. "Excuse me, excuse me," she said to the other kids as she bumped past them. The path between the trees was pretty narrow, and everyone was hiking fast, so it took her a while to reach the teacher.

"Mr. Mahoney!" she called out, when she finally caught up. "Could I ask you something? Did all this land *really* belong to Kevin's people?"

"I guess it did, a long time ago. Let's stop for a minute to catch our breaths," Mr. Mahoney suggested, although he was the only one breathing hard. But then, he was carrying the heaviest backpack. It was filled with lots of books about trees.

When he stopped suddenly, all the kids piled up behind him like a traffic jam at a red light. Mr. Mahoney turned around to face them. "Kevin, Caitlin was asking about your ancestors. Why don't you tell us about them being here long ago?"

Kevin looked down at the ground. To get him started, Caitlin asked, "How long ago?"

"A thousand years."

"What were they called?" Joe Daniel asked.

"The ancient ones," Kevin answered.

Mr. Mahoney cleared his throat. "I think . . . also . . ." he began, "they were called Fremont Indians. At least that's what today's scientists named the people who lived here then."

Kevin shrugged. "Whatever you call them, I know that this land was sacred. It was a holy place."

Mr. Mahoney waited for Kevin to continue, but when he didn't, the teacher said, "I can understand that. It really is beautiful here. So many different kinds of trees . . . look at this one overhead. Does anyone know what kind of pine this is?"

He went on to talk about the different kinds of pine

trees. One was called lodgepole pine because Indians had used it to hold up tepees. Another kind, the jack pine, was interesting because it only dropped its seeds when the forest was on fire.

Suddenly Caitlin heard a scraping sound behind her. It was a soft sound, like a dog scratching on a faraway door. She turned to see what it was, but all she could see were boulders, more pine trees, and little patches of lake shimmering in the distance.

No one but Caitlin seemed to hear the strange sound. Maybe it was because the other kids knew how to pay attention. Joe Daniel, Lily, Pablo, and Kevin watched with interest as the teacher talked, twirling a pinecone between his fingers.

Scritch-scratch-scritch-scratch. What could it be? Caitlin tried to concentrate on the pinecone in Mr. Mahoney's hand, but the soft noise kept teasing her. She turned around and looked again. The sound seemed to come from behind a large boulder not too far from them.

"A pine tree's seeds grow inside its cones," Mr. Mahoney said.

Caitlin didn't want to interrupt her teacher. But she *had* to find out what was making that curious sound!

CHAPTER
3

Caitlin took one backward step, and then another. With her eyes locked on Mr. Mahoney, she kept on walking backward toward the boulder. Step, step, step. She almost stumbled as she backed around the big granite rock. When she turned she saw—Reese Borden! Caitlin hadn't even noticed that he wasn't with the rest of the group.

"Get lost, Caitlin," Reese hissed. He was squatting on the ground with a small stick in his hand. Clumps of dirt shot into the air as he scraped the stick through the dry earth. Dust and tiny pebbles covered his expensive sneakers. Caitlin wondered if Reese's mother would get mad when she saw what Reese had done to his brand-new shoes.

"Reese, you're supposed to be listening to Mr. Mahoney," she told him.

"I'm busy," Reese snapped.

"Did you find something?"

"Maybe. If I did, it's *mine*. Why don't you go back to the class before they start looking for you?"

"I don't have to go if I don't want to. What did you

find? Buried treasure?" A buried treasure *was* more exciting than pinecones. Maybe Reese had stumbled on a bag of old gold coins or a lost diamond necklace! "Can I see?"

"Nope. Finder's keepers, and I'm a finder. Go away, Caitlin. Go learn about trees." Without looking up, Reese waved her off with a dirty hand.

The sun beat down on top of Caitlin's head, making a warm spot that spread across her scalp. She stood, unwilling to move. She should be listening to her teacher, but she couldn't leave Reese. He'd found something amazing. She knew it! But Reese just ignored her and kept digging.

"Listen, Mr. Mahoney said we shouldn't disturb anything," Caitlin told him.

Throwing down the stick, Reese began to smooth away the dirt very carefully with his fingers. "I *said* go away!" And then, as if to himself, he muttered, "I've almost got it . . . it's caught under this root. . . ." Suddenly Reese flew backward and thumped onto his bottom. Something dirt-covered, something shaped sort of like a carrot, was clutched in his hand. Caitlin couldn't help but feel a little disappointed. Whatever Reese had found didn't look like much.

". . . leaves make sugar. Sugar feeds the tree." Mr. Mahoney's voice floated over them. "Excuse me, kids, we seem to be missing two members of our science club. Reese? Caitlin? Where are you?"

A fierce scowl pulled down the corners of Reese's

mouth. "Now you've done it, Caitlin," he said. "Here comes the whole group. Thanks a lot!"

"Caitlin? Reese?" Mr. Mahoney shouted, louder this time.

"We're over here! Behind the rock!" Caitlin called back.

Caitlin heard the rustle of footsteps and the crack of fallen branches as the Science Club members gathered around them. Joe Daniel frowned. His arms were crossed, which meant he wasn't very happy. He didn't like it when Mr. Mahoney got interrupted. Joe Daniel wanted to be a science teacher someday, so he always paid attention when Mr. Mahoney talked.

"What are you guys up to?" Mr. Mahoney asked. "You know you're not supposed to leave the group."

"I'm sorry, Mr. Mahoney. It's just that Reese found something buried in the dirt, and I wanted to see what it was," Caitlin answered quickly.

"Buried? You mean you dug it up?" Mr. Mahoney frowned, but Reese just stared at the ground. "You know the rules, Reese. You don't disturb anything on public land. What have you got there? Show me."

Reese held his right hand behind his back. "Nothing," he muttered.

"Reese, if you've found something, I need to know about it. Now."

Slowly Reese pulled his hand from behind him. Caitlin strained to see. All the kids in the club leaned forward.

Mr. Mahoney gently lifted the dark object from

Reese's hand. Carefully he brushed dirt from it. He turned it slowly and squinted. Then, suddenly, his eyes got wide. "Oh, my word!" Mr. Mahoney said excitedly. "Reese, do you know what you've found? You've made an incredible discovery! This is a Fremont Indian statue! It's very valuable!"

"It is?" Caitlin said out loud.

"Looks like an old piece of rock," Pablo snorted. "I've got a load of them in my backyard I can sell you."

"No, no, Pablo, this isn't a rock!" Mr. Mahoney shook his head. "It's a figure made of gray clay. See the head here? And the eyes?"

The teacher held up the small statue so that everyone could see it. It was only about four inches tall. The eyes were narrow slits. The broad shoulders tapered down to narrow hips, and the little figure seemed to be wearing a fancy headdress and a necklace.

"This clay figure is probably a thousand years old!" Mr. Mahoney exclaimed. "How did you find it, Reese?"

"I saw a little bit of the end sticking up, and I started digging." Reese held out his hand to Mr. Mahoney. "Excuse me, but I found it and that makes it mine. Give it back, please."

Suddenly Kevin Running Fox pushed through the group until he was standing right in front of Reese. His dark eyebrows scrunched together so that they almost met in the middle.

"Reese, you need to put the statue back where you

found it," Kevin said. "You never should have dug it up."

"Well, I did, so big deal!"

"Put it back!" Kevin stood as if his feet had grown into the earth. He didn't move, not even when Reese stepped so close that they were standing eye to eye.

Mr. Mahoney moved between the two angry boys. "There's nothing to argue about. This statue isn't going anywhere. We'll leave it right where you found it, Reese, and we'll notify the Forest Service."

"Hey! That's not fair!" Reese howled.

Mr. Mahoney just shook his head. "That's the law, and that's the way it's got to be. Reese, all of you kids, try to understand. Have you ever tried to put together a jigsaw puzzle when some of the pieces were missing?"

Caitlin nodded. Sometimes she and her mom went to garage sales and bought puzzles for twenty-five cents. It always made her mad when some of the pieces were gone. Then the whole picture was ruined.

"Well, this clay figure is like a puzzle piece that will help make a picture of how the Fremont people lived long ago," Mr. Mahoney explained. "Taking it away would ruin the whole picture for the scientists who study the past. Those scientists are called archaeologists."

"If we leave it," Lily wanted to know, "how will the forest rangers know where to find it?"

"I'll stop at Forest Service headquarters and tell them where it is," Mr. Mahoney said.

"I know what we can do!" Pablo suggested. "Let's make a circle of rocks around it. It's okay to do that, isn't it, Mr. Mahoney? Just move a few rocks to mark the spot?"

"And I'll leave my red bandanna on top of it," Joe Daniel offered. "Red is the easiest color to spot in a forest." He reached into his backpack, took out the bandanna, and removed a rubber band from it. Inside were half a dozen pens and pencils.

"Okay, I'm going to put the statue back now, Reese," Mr. Mahoney stated. Scowling, Reese watched as Mr. Mahoney fitted the figure back into the hollow it had left in the dirt.

Pablo built a small circle of rocks. Gently, Joe Daniel laid his red bandanna on top of the figure.

"There! Now let's write down the exact directions for the Forest Service people," Mr. Mahoney said. "We'll count the footsteps from here to that really tall lodgepole pine."

Everyone got excited about counting the footsteps. "Twelve, thirteen . . ."

"Sixteen, seventeen, eighteen . . ."

"I'm only up to fifteen."

"That's because you have big feet!"

Next they counted the trees from the clearing to the lake. Then they counted them once more, just so the forest rangers couldn't possibly miss their wonderful find. When they'd finished, all the kids felt so good about themselves that they smacked palms together and yelled, "Way to go, Three Peaks Science Club!"

CHAPTER
4

Mr. Stan Wiley was waiting at the shore. "You're a lot later than you said you'd be," he complained.

"That's because I made a really important find," Reese bragged. "I found a little Indian statue."

"That so?" Mr. Wiley asked.

"It's worth a lot of money. But Mr. Mahoney wouldn't let me keep it. He made me put it back!"

Squinting into the trees, Mr. Wiley said, "You know, all this land over here used to belong to my family. Well, maybe we didn't exactly own it, but we grazed cattle here till the government made us stop. Funny we never found any Indian relics in all those years."

"It was just a little way down the trail," Caitlin began. "Joe Daniel Giles left his bandanna there so the Forest Service people can find the statue."

Mr. Wiley took off his cowboy hat and wiped his brow. His forehead was very white where the hat had covered it. The rest of his face was red from sunburn. It wasn't an especially nice-looking face, Caitlin thought.

"Joe Daniel Giles. Would that be Ralph Giles's grandson?" Mr. Wiley asked Caitlin.

"That's right."

"Which boy is he? Point him out to me."

Caitlin looked around. "He's the one handing out the life jackets."

Mr. Mahoney was shouting, "Kids, make sure you have everything you brought with you—sweaters, papers, candy wrappers. Remember, 'When on government land, take nothing away except memories. Leave nothing behind . . .'"

"Except footprints," all the kids finished together. They knew the saying by heart.

"Okay, then, buckle your life jackets and get into the boats."

The trip back across the lake seemed to go a lot faster than the trip over. They'd barely climbed out of the boats when they saw a cloud of dust rise up on the dirt road that led to the Wiley ranch.

"Here comes the first parent," Mr. Mahoney announced. "I think it's your mom, Caitlin. Kids, make sure you have all your belongings." He shouted that last part because Caitlin's mother's car made so much racket as it clattered up the road. The old car rattled like a tin can full of marbles.

When it came to a stop, Caitlin's mother rolled down the window on the driver's side.

"Hi, Mrs. Marsh," Mr. Mahoney said.

"Hello, Mr. Mahoney. Hi, Caitlin. Hi, everyone," Caitlin's mother, April Marsh, called out. Then she said, "Joe Daniel, your grandpa's truck wouldn't start, and he asked me to drive you home. I've got some packages on the front seat, so you and Caitlin can sit in the back."

Joe Daniel didn't say anything. He just got in the back, beside Caitlin.

Caitlin couldn't wait to tell her mother the news. "Mom, guess what!" She had to shout because, even from the inside, the car rattled as it bumped back down the road.

"What?"

"Reese Borden found an ancient Indian statue in the dirt. It's worth a huge amount of money. Maybe even a hundred dollars!"

"More like ten thousand," Joe Daniel scoffed.

"Ten thousand—"

"Dollars!" Joe Daniel finished. "Didn't you hear Mr. Mahoney talking about it?"

Caitlin swallowed hard, remembering that she'd touched the statue. Taken it from Reese's hand. Held it in her own hand—something worth ten thousand dollars! What if she'd dropped it?

"Wow!" Caitlin's mother exclaimed from the front seat. "For ten thousand dollars, I could have a nice new car instead of this old rattletrap."

"At least your car runs," Joe Daniel said to Caitlin. "My grandpa can hardly get our old truck to start anymore. If I had ten thousand dollars . . ." His voice trailed off.

"What would you do?" Caitlin asked. She really

wanted to know. It wasn't often that Joe Daniel talked to her the way he was now. Maybe it was because, right at that moment, none of his friends were around to see him with a third-grade girl.

"If I had that statue, I'd sell it and buy my grandpa a pickup truck. A big, rugged truck that could go anywhere."

"Joe Daniel . . ." Caitlin murmured. She didn't know quite how to make the words come out right. "Wouldn't it be . . . wrong . . . to sell the statue? Kevin says it was special to the ancient people. It was part of their religion. Kevin says, how would you like it if people came and dug up your ancestors right out of the cemetery? People who are looking for pots and arrowheads and baskets and things do that to old Indian graveyards all the time."

"When did he tell you all that?" Joe Daniel asked.

"On the way back in the rowboat."

Joe Daniel rubbed his chin. "Yeah, I guess Kevin's right."

"Besides, selling the Indian statue would bring bad luck," Caitlin added. "Kevin says the spirits would get so angry, they'd cause *big* trouble."

"Do you believe that?" Joe Daniel asked. From the look on his face, she could tell that he didn't.

"I'm not sure," she said.

"Well, I'm sure," Joe Daniel told her. "Spirits don't make trouble. *People* make trouble."

At that moment, Caitlin couldn't have imagined just how much trouble there was going to be.

CHAPTER
5

Three Peaks wasn't a big place. You could park your car and walk a few blocks to just about anywhere in town.

"Kids, I have to get to the post office before it closes," Caitlin's mother said. Her mother made a living by knitting ski hats. At least once a week, she had to mail a bundle of hats to ski resorts in faraway places.

"You said you needed to buy some things for school, Caitlin," she continued. "Here's three dollars. Is that enough?"

Caitlin nodded. "Want to come with me, Joe Daniel?" she asked.

Joe Daniel scrunched up his eyebrows. Whenever he did that, Caitlin knew she wasn't going to like his answer, because that's how he looked when he didn't want to hurt her feelings. "Uh . . . I think I'll just check out the trucks in the used-car lot," he said.

Caitlin wasn't too surprised that Joe Daniel didn't want to go shopping with her. She tucked the money her mother had given her into the pocket of her jeans.

Then Caitlin, her mother, and Joe Daniel all walked off in different directions.

In Yokum's Variety Store, Caitlin bought a ruler, a tablet with lines, and a six-inch-long, two-inch-wide pink rubber eraser. Stamped in black on the eraser were the words "For BIG Misteaks." Caitlin grinned at the joke. She knew how "mistakes" was really spelled.

At a different store, Caitlin looked around carefully for a long time, and then made one very special purchase. With the last and best purchase clamped under her arm, she waited beside the car for her mother and Joe Daniel.

"Did you get everything you needed?" her mother asked when they were almost home. They'd already dropped off Joe Daniel at the Giles ranch, and their car was bumping down the dusty hill to Three Peaks Trailer Court.

"Yep. Did you?"

"Uh-huh. After the post office, I stopped for groceries. We're having meatloaf for dinner tonight."

Caitlin smiled. Meatloaf was her favorite.

Inside their trailer, she gathered up all her bags and took them to her room. Hers was the very last room in the trailer, the room on the end. Through her wide back window, Caitlin could see the three Rocky Mountain peaks that gave their name to everything around her: the trailer court, the school she went to, the town the school was in, and the lodge and ski resort where most of the townspeople worked.

She climbed onto her bed and sat cross-legged, then reached inside a bag marked "Three Peaks Bookstore" and pulled out a large paperback book. With her thumbnail, she scraped off the price sticker: "$5.95" had been crossed out on the sticker. "$4.95" had been written in and crossed out; "$3.00" and then "$2.00" and "$1.50" had all been crossed out with red ink. Caitlin knew how to shop for bargains, all right. Her mother had taught her, because they had to stretch their money further than most people had to.

"One dollar!" Caitlin said triumphantly. She'd spent her last dollar on a paperback book about American Indians.

She paged through the book, looking at drawings of Indian men and boys hunting alone and in groups, hurling spears at bighorn sheep, shooting deer with bows and arrows. Other pictures showed women sewing moccasins from deer hides and molding clay. The women in the book were making pots, not little statues, but Caitlin imagined they would have used the same kind of clay.

She closed her eyes to think about brown-skinned families living around Three Peaks a thousand years ago, hunting, feeding their children, telling stories around a fire—leaving behind one perfect clay statue that, a thousand years later, Reese Borden had found.

If the spirits of the ancient people were still around, why did they pick bratty Reese, of all people, to find the statue? They could have picked Caitlin, who always tried to be nice to everyone. She sighed. It

didn't seem fair. But maybe there was *something* good about Reese, something buried deep inside him, so deep that only the spirits could see it. If there were such things as spirits. Were spirits something like angels? It was hard to figure out.

After dinner, Caitlin put on her pajamas and curled up on her bed again with her new book. Before she could read very much, though, she found herself falling asleep. She flopped back onto her pillow with the book covering her face.

Caitlin woke up with a start. She didn't know what had roused her. The book lay beside her on the pillow.

A huge, bright moon shone through the window, making shadows all over her bedroom. Caitlin held her breath. She'd never before seen a moon that big. Or that bright.

The night was quiet. Very quiet. An owl hooted, startling her. She heard rustling, and a sound like voices sighing. That had to be the wind. Or could it be the spirits of those long-dead Indians, sad because Reese dug up their statue?

Then she heard a cracking noise, as though a large animal were stepping on twigs as it hurried through the brush. And heavy breathing. Again it sounded like something big—a deer or a mountain sheep.

Caitlin knew she should get up and look out the window, but she was afraid. What if it really *was* spirits? She pulled the covers over her head and almost instantly began to dream of warriors chasing her and Joe Daniel through the forest.

CHAPTER

6

An Indian spirit floated through Mr. Mahoney's reading room.

It wasn't really true, but Caitlin almost believed it was. During library time, Mr. Mahoney always sat perched on top of his special reading stool, a book held in his hands. Today he spoke in a hoarse, whispery voice that rose and fell eerily. It made the story seem so real that everyone in the combined third- and fourth-grade reading class stayed quiet. Even Reese Borden sat still and paid attention.

Not a foot scraped on the floor, not a chair squeaked as Mr. Mahoney read them the story of an Indian girl who drowned in a lake and haunted a family through a cracked basin. Caitlin felt her skin bump up in shivery gooseflesh.

From the corner of her eye, she saw a fluttery movement at the library door. A face appeared, pressed against the small pane of glass. Then it disappeared, and appeared again. For a second, Caitlin thought it might be one of the ancient Indian spirits. Then she remembered that she was in Mr.

Mahoney's reading room in the Three Peaks School, not in a dark forest. Still, she jumped halfway out of her seat when someone tapped gently on the door.

"Mr. Mahoney," Caitlin interrupted. "Somebody's here."

Dropping the book into his lap, Mr. Mahoney, changing from his storytelling voice to his regular voice, said, "Yes! Hello!" He waved the person inside. "Please, come in."

A tall young woman slipped into the room. "Sorry to break into your story time," she said. The woman's heavy boots clopped across the floor. She was dressed in a green uniform with a badge on the sleeve. In the center of the badge were the letters "U.S." with a pine tree stitched between them. Above that were the words "Forest Service."

She held out her hand to Mr. Mahoney as she introduced herself. "I'm Jane Tandy, a conservation officer with the Forest Service. I need to speak to you about the Fremont statue your Science Club found."

Mr. Mahoney stood up to shake hands with the woman. "Oh, yes!" he said enthusiastically. "Could you follow the directions I left at your office? We marked the site with a ring of rocks and a red bandanna."

Officer Tandy nodded. "Your directions were fine. We were able to find those markers."

"Wonderful!" Mr. Mahoney looked pleased. "It's great that our Science Club uncovered a valuable piece of pre-American history."

Homework for
tomorrow:
Math Bk. Pgs
56-58
Book Repo
Due

"Yeah? Except the Science Club didn't find it," Reese complained loudly. "*I* did! And it should have been finder's keepers."

Mr. Mahoney sighed. "Yes, Reese, we know that's how you feel. Why don't you stand up so Ms. Tandy can see the person who actually made the find."

Tossing his head to throw his blond hair out of his eyes, Reese stood up. He gave a little bow. Then he gave a second bow, almost as if he were waiting for applause.

"That's enough, Reese." Mr. Mahoney signaled for Reese to sit down and keep quiet. But Reese kept bowing. "Reese, sit!" Mr. Mahoney ordered. "*Now!*"

Some of the kids started to giggle. It *was* kind of funny, in an obnoxious sort of way, Caitlin thought, that Reese wouldn't stop showing off. But Officer Tandy didn't smile. In fact, she looked grim.

"I'm sorry, but we have a problem," she said. Leaning toward Mr. Mahoney, she said something in a voice so soft that Caitlin couldn't make out the words.

"Are you sure?" he cried.

"Positive," Officer Tandy answered. She leaned even closer and said something more.

"But—but . . . this doesn't make any sense," Mr. Mahoney stuttered. "There has to be some mistake."

"There's no mistake. We checked everywhere."

What was going on? Caitlin wondered. Whatever it was, she could tell it wasn't good.

Mr. Mahoney yanked his fingers through his hair. He looked very worried. "Class, I'm sorry, but I'll have to step out for a moment. I'll send someone from the office to be with you until I get back." He frowned, then pushed his wire-framed glasses back in place. "Will the following students please come with me?" With his index finger, he pointed to where each of them sat. "Reese Borden," he said. "Kevin Running Fox. Lily Kato. And Caitlin Marsh."

"Me?" Caitlin's heart squeezed in her chest. "What is it, Mr. Mahoney?" she cried. "What happened?"

"You kids might as well know," Officer Tandy answered. "We found your circle of rocks. We found the red bandanna. We even found an imprint the statue had left in the dirt. But we couldn't find the statue. An archaeologist and I dug all around the site this morning. The Fremont statue is gone."

"What?" Lily cried. "We all saw it!"

The officer shook her head. "We believe you. We're sure the statue *was* there. But it's missing now. And it's my job to find out who took it!"

CHAPTER

7

"Mr. Mahoney, are we in trouble?" Caitlin asked.

"No."

"Then why are we in the teachers' lounge? I've never been in here before."

"We can talk here."

"Oh. You know what, Mr. Mahoney? I thought the lounge would look more interesting than this, but it's so plain. I thought there'd be a television in here. I like all the windows you have, though. There's a big puddle of water outside. Did you see it? It's like a tiny lake—"

"Caitlin, please."

Caitlin felt herself blush. She was nervous, and whenever she got nervous, she talked as fast as the birds that chattered outside her window every morning. Sometimes her mother teased her and called her "Caitlin Magpie." Ducking her head, she clamped her mouth shut.

"Am I supposed to come in here?" Joe Daniel Giles opened the door and stepped inside.

"Yes, come in, Joe Daniel. Good. Pablo's with you."

Turning toward Officer Tandy, Mr. Mahoney stated, "We're all here now—all the club members who were on the field trip yesterday."

Mr. Mahoney's voice remained calm, but his forehead was wrinkled with concern. To Joe Daniel and Pablo he explained, "I guess you're wondering why you've been called out of class. The Fremont statue we discovered yesterday is missing. This is Ms. Tandy, and she wants to ask the Science Club members a few questions."

"Why don't we sit down?" Jane Tandy suggested. Mr. Mahoney gestured to a table where the teachers ate lunch every day.

Joe Daniel sank into the closest empty chair. Caitlin was glad it happened to be next to her. He smelled the way he always did—like Tide laundry soap mixed with a hint of cinnamon, which was the kind of gum he liked best.

"Let's begin at the beginning," Officer Tandy said. "Reese, you were the one who found the statue."

"Yeah." Reese shrugged his shoulders. "But that doesn't mean I stole it."

"No, of course it doesn't," the woman answered. "But I heard what you said—'finder's keepers.' Maybe you felt that it should have been yours to keep."

"Listen," Reese said, "I learned something a long time ago when I started making movies. Life's not fair." He slid down in his seat and crossed his arms. "I can deal with that. I mean, why would I want to take some old clay statue?"

"Because it's worth about ten thousand dollars, that's why," Pablo declared.

"Yeah, well, I can earn that in a day." Reese pointed a finger at Pablo. "You're always playing jokes. Maybe you took it to be funny."

"Reese Borden," Pablo snorted, "you must have a really tiny brain. When I left the forest, I was walking with Lily Kato. No way could I have taken the statue."

"That's true," Lily said. "He was with me. We were talking about snakes. Pablo said there were pine snakes that dropped out of pine trees onto people's heads."

"I made that up just to scare her," Pablo admitted, grinning.

Reese raised an eyebrow at Officer Tandy and told her, "Maybe you should ask Kevin Running Fox. He said the statue really belonged to his people. Maybe he buried it somewhere so no one else could find it."

His voice squeaking, Kevin cried, "Me! You're crazy, Reese! I'd never even touch something that sacred. I don't want the spirits getting mad at me!"

Reese snorted. "Yeah. Sure. Blame it on the spirits."

Caitlin broke in, "Hey, maybe Kevin's right. I heard strange sounds outside my window last night. Maybe the spirits *were* angry."

"Oh? What time did you hear these noises?" Officer Tandy asked.

Caitlin squinted at the ceiling and murmured, "I'm not sure exactly what time it was. All I know is that the moon was really bright. That's when I heard something. First it was like whispers. I thought it was the wind. Then it sounded like an animal crashing along the ground, right outside my window."

Jane Tandy leaned toward Caitlin and stared right into her eyes. "Can you describe the sounds?" she asked.

"I . . . I don't know." Caitlin frowned, trying to remember. "Like . . . a deer, or something big, breathing hard. And hooves . . . But I'm not even sure I was awake. I might have been dreaming."

"You live close to Joe Daniel Giles, don't you?" the woman asked Caitlin.

"He lives at the top of the road and I live at the bottom. It only takes ten minutes to walk from the Giles ranch house to our trailer—I mean, if I'm going down the hill. Going up the hill takes longer." Caitlin had begun chattering again. She felt very nervous. Beside her, Joe Daniel looked like he wanted to say something, if Caitlin would just stop talking.

No one heard a knock, but the door swung open. Sheriff George Garett, wearing his ten-gallon cowboy hat, filled the doorway. "Just stay where you are," he told them.

CHAPTER

8

"**W**hich one of you is Joe Daniel Giles?" the sheriff asked in a loud voice. Caitlin could feel Joe Daniel stiffen in the seat next to her.

"I'm Joe Daniel Giles," he answered.

Sheriff Garett squinted his eyes at Joe Daniel. "You the boy who was looking at a pickup truck for your grandpa yesterday?"

"Yes, sir."

"You have the money to buy a truck like that?"

"No, sir. I was just looking."

"Excuse me, but I don't understand what's going on here," Mr. Mahoney said, rising to his feet. "I'm the teacher who took the Science Club on the field trip. Can I help you?"

"Nope. I just have a few questions for the boy. If you just sit tight, I might be able to clear this up fast." To Joe Daniel, Sheriff Garett said, "Guess you wanted a truck real bad, didn't you, Joe Daniel? Bad enough to steal that Fremont Indian statue."

"I didn't do anything wrong!" Joe Daniel kept his eyes on the sheriff, but his fingers were knotted tightly together on the tabletop.

"I'd like to believe that. I know your grandpa. We were in school together. I know how he took you in when your parents died and raised you like a son. For that reason, I'm willing to walk out of this room if you'll be straight with me. How 'bout it?"

"I *am* being straight!" Joe Daniel insisted.

Lily, Kevin, Reese, and Pablo sat as still as statues, with wide, scared eyes. Caitlin fidgeted in her seat, and Joe Daniel just stared at the sheriff as if he couldn't believe this was happening.

Sheriff Garett squeezed the bridge of his nose and shut his eyes. He sighed. "Kids today don't understand that just because they want something real bad, that doesn't mean they can up and take it. Thirty-three years as a sheriff in a little town like Three Peaks, and you think you get to know how people will act. I never would have believed that Ralph Giles's grandson would do anything bad. But there's an eyewitness—"

"What?" Mr. Mahoney cried. "An eyewitness? Are you trying to say that someone saw Joe Daniel take the clay figure?"

"I'm not trying to say it, Mr. Mahoney. I *am* saying it. I'm also saying it would go a whole lot easier on this boy if he just hands over the Fremont figure."

"I don't have it!" Joe Daniel cried.

"Then what did you do with it?"

"Nothing! I never had it! I never even touched it yesterday when Reese found it!"

45

"That so?" Sheriff Garett took off his hat and ran the brim between his fingers. "Well, Joe Daniel, Mr. Stan Wiley says you did. He swears he saw your horse tied up at the dock last night. He says he saw you take a rowboat and paddle across the lake at one o'clock in the morning. Says he was standing on the porch of his ranch house, and he saw you clear as day."

"What! No way!" Joe Daniel cried.

The sheriff leaned his knuckles on the table. "From what Stan Wiley says, you were rowing right along the path of the moon's reflection on the water. Wiley says that strip of moonlight lit you up like a searchlight. He's positive it was you, because he got out his binoculars to take a good look. So what do you have to say for yourself now?"

Leaping from her seat, Caitlin cried, "That Mr. Wiley is a great big liar!" Caitlin couldn't believe the words she heard coming from her very own mouth. She'd never called anyone a liar before, especially not a grown-up! And the person she was telling it to was a sheriff with a shiny silver badge!

But for Mr. Wiley to call Joe Daniel a thief, Caitlin knew that *had* to be a lie. Joe Daniel would never take a penny that didn't belong to him.

"Caitlin, sit down!" Joe Daniel hissed. He pulled on her shirtsleeve, but Caitlin stood like a rock.

"And who are you, young lady?" Sheriff Garett asked calmly.

"Caitlin Marsh." Now that Sheriff Garett was staring at her, Caitlin's voice began to quiver a little.

"Well, Caitlin Marsh, I'd say you're a loyal friend. But you need to understand that the Fremont statue is worth a lot of money. That makes stealing it a felony. Plus it's a federal offense because it was on federal land."

Caitlin stared right back at the sheriff. "If Joe Daniel says he didn't take it, then he didn't," she declared. "He's the most honest person in this whole school!"

"Stop it, Caitlin. Just *sit down*!" Joe Daniel insisted.

But Caitlin wouldn't stop. "One time Joe Daniel found a five-dollar bill in the lunchroom. He asked every single kid in school if the money belonged to them, and then he asked all the teachers. And when no one said yes, Joe Daniel still wouldn't keep it! He donated the money to Save the Whales."

Officer Tandy had been marking things in a notebook. Now she stood up and said, "I'd like to ask a question. Caitlin, didn't you tell me you heard a sound in the middle of the night?"

"Yes. I thought it might be Indian spirits." Caitlin's eyes grew bigger. "Do you think the spirits came back and took the statue?"

Officer Tandy smiled and shook her head. "I think the spirits have better things to do, Caitlin. I'm wondering about that other sound you heard—the sound of a large animal. Maybe it was Joe Daniel's horse. He could have ridden past your trailer on the way to the lake."

This time it was Joe Daniel who jumped to his feet.

to the table. "Let's start by drawing a map."

"Why?" Reese asked. "What good is a map? We already know where the statue was."

"Maps keep things straight in your head." Pablo tore a sheet of paper out of his notebook. "Give me a pencil, Reese. Now let's work on this."

"The lake's shaped sort of like a long potato," Kevin began.

"Okay." Pablo drew it. "And Mr. Wiley's ranch house is right here, up at the north end of the lake." He made an X.

Getting into the spirit of things, Lily said, "Put another X where the dock is."

Officer Tandy added, "The moon rose in the east last night, right about . . . there!" She pointed with her pen to the east rim of the lake. Pablo drew a moon there.

"Sit down, Caitlin, and help us," Mr. Mahoney suggested.

"I can't! I can't sit still!" She paced back and forth, back and forth, in front of the windows in the teacher's lounge. She was scowling because she was worrying so hard as she paced and stared out the windows.

The recent rainstorm had left a wide puddle of water, about an inch deep, on the flat roof of the building next door. That was the school's gym. From where she paced, on the second floor of the school's main building, Caitlin could see down onto the gym roof, where water always collected after a rainstorm.

She stopped and stared at the puddle, where the afternoon sun reflected. . . .

She stared harder, frowned, and walked along the wall of the teachers' lounge, looking out the windows as she walked. Then she walked all the way back in the other direction, peering out again as she passed each window. She never took her eyes off the sun's reflection in the big puddle on the adjoining roof.

"Let me see that map!" she cried. Running to where Pablo sat, she tore the map out of his hands.

"Joe Daniel is innocent!" she shouted. "Mr. Wiley lied! And I can prove it!"

CHAPTER 10

"I'm sorry," the large lady said, "but children can't go in there. Sheriff Garett is busy. You kids will just have to wait. And why are you carrying that tub of water? You plan on giving the sheriff a bath?" Her laugh sounded like a blast from a horn. "Or do you think it's his birthday, since you got a candle stuck in the tub?"

The galvanized tub was heavy. Caitlin held it by the handle on one side and Kevin held it on the other side. Since Kevin was taller than Caitlin, the tub slanted, sloshing water sideways. Caitlin wished they could set it down before the water spilled, but she was afraid to ask permission. The big, uniformed woman looked too mean to say yes.

"We're all members of the Three Peaks Science Club," Caitlin explained. Since she had to hold the tub with both hands, she twisted her head to point out the other club members. "That's Pablo Miramontes, and Reese Borden, and Lily Kato, and Kevin's holding the other side of this tub, and Mr. Mahoney's trying to find a place to park his station wagon. . . ."

"I don't care if you're all the queen of England," the woman declared. "You have to leave."

The strain of holding the heavy tub made Caitlin's voice squeak. "We need to help our friend Joe Daniel. We brought this tub with the candle stuck in the middle to prove—"

The woman cut Caitlin off. "Forget it. Besides, that Joe Daniel deserves the trouble he's in. And don't slop any of that water on my floor!" Crossing her arms over her chest, the woman scowled down at them.

"Please, can't we go inside?" Caitlin begged.

"Not a chance!"

There was no way to get around this huge woman. She looked as though her feet had been glued to the shabby, mud-colored floor tiles. Caitlin could hear the murmur of grown-up voices inside. She *had* to get in there and help Joe Daniel!

Suddenly Reese circled around from behind Kevin. He walked right up in front of the big woman, and he smiled at her. Even though Reese was kind of short, he managed to stand so that every inch of him counted.

"Hi," he said.

"Hi yourself."

"Do you know who I am?" he asked.

The woman squinted at Reese. "I don't know. But you look familiar. Are you my cousin Betsy's kid?" Bending down, she peered at Reese more closely. "Wait a minute," she said. "I *do* recognize you."

"You might have seen me in my latest movie, *Ninja Hero*. What's your name?"

"Me?" Suddenly the woman looked shy. "I'm Zelda Bennett."

"Hello, Zelda. It's nice to meet you. I'm Reese Borden."

Smacking her palm into her forehead, Zelda said, "Yes! Of course! Reese Borden! Oh, my gosh, I can't believe it! Reese Borden, the movie star!" Zelda's eyebrows shot halfway up her forehead. A smile as big as her feet crossed her face.

Reese cleared his throat. "Zelda, I hate to ask you to bend the rules, but would you please let us inside? I can tell that someone as nice as you wouldn't stand in the way of justice. And this really is *very* important."

"Oh," Zelda said, flushing, "I don't . . ."

"And when we come out, I'll give you my autograph. I'll sign it, 'To my good friend Zelda Bennett. With love, Reese Borden.'"

"Well . . ." Zelda wavered.

"And I'll give you some free tickets to *Ninja Hero*. It's playing right now at the Three Peaks Cinema. How 'bout it?"

"Okay! Yes!" Zelda reached around to open the door. "But you kids have to promise to stay real quiet."

They filed silently into the back of the stuffy office, Caitlin and Kevin bumping the tub awkwardly between them. Stan Wiley, Joe Daniel, and Joe Daniel's grandfather, Ralph Giles, stood in front of the sheriff's desk. Mr. Wiley was talking loudly, his face as red as a cherry, his fist balled into a thick knot.

"I saw him. I did! In the moonlight, clear as day! I saw that boy Joe Daniel row across the lake, with the moonlight lighting him up like a lantern. I watched him from my porch. I'd stake my life on the fact that it was that boy. If some Indian statue is missing, then arrest that young hooligan. Don't come bothering me!"

"I didn't take anything!" Joe Daniel cried.

"Hush," his grandfather said.

"But I *didn't*!"

"We'll get our turn to speak," his grandfather said softly.

Suddenly the tub of water got too heavy. Caitlin couldn't hold it any longer. "I have to put this down!" she whispered to Kevin. They tried to lower it quietly, but the metal hit the floor with a clank.

"What's all this?" Sheriff Garett exclaimed. He peered around the others. "Who let you kids in here?"

Talking as fast as she could—and Caitlin was a very fast talker when she got nervous—she cried, "Mr. Wiley couldn't have seen Joe Daniel in the moon's reflection on the water!"

"Who says I couldn't?" Mr. Wiley demanded, turning around to glare at Caitlin.

"At least not if you were standing on your porch."

Mr. Mahoney's voice reached them from the door. He'd made it at last! "A light's reflection always stretches from the light's source to the eye of the viewer," he said.

"What the heck does that mean?" Stan Wiley demanded.

"My science club students would like to perform a little experiment for you folks," Mr. Mahoney answered. "Go ahead, kids."

"I get to light the candle!" Reese insisted. Caitlin was about to strike the match herself, but she hesitated. Reese could be the most obnoxious kid in all of Three Peaks, but they'd never have gotten in here if it weren't for him. She handed over the matches.

"What is all this about?" Sheriff Garett wanted to know.

"I think you'll have to get up from your chair, Sheriff," Caitlin told him. "Walk around the tub of water and watch the reflection from the burning candle."

"Yes. Well?" the sheriff asked as he circled the tub.

"Don't you notice?" Kevin asked. "The reflection from the candle's flame follows you around."

Caitlin took the sheriff's hand and walked beside him, all around the tub.

"See the path the candlelight makes on the water?" Pablo asked him. "It follows you when you circle around it."

"Moonlight on water is like a finger," Caitlin told the sheriff. "It points from the moon to the person looking at it."

"We drew this map." Kevin held it out to the sheriff.

"See," Lily said, "the moon rose here." She pointed to the circle they'd drawn on the rim of the lake. "Mr. Wiley said he was standing over there. If he was, the

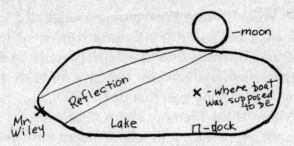

moon's reflection would have stretched all the way across the water, right into his eyes."

"Mr. Wiley said the reflection lit up Joe Daniel," Caitlin added. "But it couldn't have. Not if Joe Daniel was over here." She pointed to another X on the map.

"Caitlin said it best—moonlight on water is like a finger," Mr. Mahoney told the sheriff. "It points from the moon right to the person watching it. So Mr. Wiley couldn't have seen Joe Daniel in the moonlight's path, as he said he did."

"Well, I'll be!" Joe Daniel's grandfather walked around the tub, too. "The kids are right! It works just the way they say—the reflection follows me."

Sheriff Garett pulled himself up to his full six-foot height and glared at Mr. Wiley, who began to stammer.

"Are—are you going to believe a bunch of kids? I'm telling you what I saw, Sheriff. Anyway, those government fellows think they own everything! Bunch of Greenies! Tree huggers! I used to run cattle over on that land, and I never found so much as an arrowhead. And those Indian artifacts are worth a whole lot of money nowadays."

Mr. Wiley's voice kept getting louder and louder. "And what do you think those government fellows are gonna do with a find like that? They'll just stick it in a museum somewhere. Or give it back to the Indians. What good will that do?"

"Where is the Fremont statue?" The sheriff spoke softly, but everyone could tell he meant business.

Suddenly meek, Stan Wiley replied, "It's in the glove compartment of my truck. I wrapped it up in a towel. Want me to go get it?"

"Wait a minute," Joe Daniel's grandfather said. "How come you blamed my grandson? Was it because you're mad at me?"

"Yes, I'm mad!" Mr. Wiley sputtered. "I should have won that court case instead of you!" He turned to the sheriff and said, "We've been feuding over a boundary line for years. Last week the judge ruled in Ralph Giles's favor."

Sheriff Garett shook his head. "You're a mean, spiteful person, Stan Wiley," he said. "The law's going to come down on you real hard."

CHAPTER

11

It was their final field trip before winter. This time the Three Peaks Science Club was studying rocks near a quarry in Three Peaks Canyon.

At the base of a cluster of maple trees, Joe Daniel stretched out on the ground. His feet rested against the large wicker basket he'd brought with him.

"What's in there?" Caitlin asked. "Can I see?" She lifted a red-and-white-checked towel from the top of the basket.

"They're pies. My grandma made them for the Science Club," Joe Daniel answered. "You can take them out."

Carefully Caitlin lifted out one pie, then another, and then a third.

"Cherry," Joe Daniel said. "My favorite kind."

Kevin Running Fox rubbed his hand across his stomach. "Look, there's a pie for each of us—Caitlin, me, and Joe Daniel. We'll eat them before the other kids see," he joked.

"No way! I'll eat all three," Caitlin teased back. "I found them, and that makes them all mine! Finder's

keepers! Remember? That's what Reese said when he found the statue."

Suddenly Caitlin grew serious. She thought about what had happened that day when Reese had tried to claim the statue as his own. She looked at Kevin. "Could I ask you something?"

"Sure. What?"

"I was just wondering. How do you feel about the clay statue?"

"You mean now that it's in the Tribal Council Museum?"

Caitlin nodded.

"I feel good about it." With a stick, Kevin drew a figure in the dust at his feet, a figure with wide shoulders, a headdress, and a necklace. "Everyone who sees it there will know that even a thousand years ago, my people made beautiful things."

"What about the spirits?" Caitlin asked. "Do you think they got angry?"

Just then, a soft wind blew over them, rising into the trees to spin orange and gold leaves all around them. One perfect maple leaf, yellow in the center and bright red on its edges, dropped into Caitlin's lap, like a gift.

Kevin didn't answer her question, but he smiled.

"I guess they didn't," Caitlin said. She lifted the lovely maple leaf into the sunlight to admire it. "I'm really glad."